To:

From:

LUCIE + POMPETTE

To request permission please contact the publisher at bonjour@lucieandpompette.com

Hardcover: ISBN: 978-0-578-93347-4

Lucie + Pompette
Rancho Mirage, Ca. 92270
www.lucieandpompette.com

The Heiress from Paris

and her lip gloss dream

Written and Illustrated by

Eric Sakas

In a Grand *Château* in the heart of Paris
there lived a *Chic* and lovely heiress.

Her name was Lucie
and she lived with her pet,
a *very* French poodle
she called Pompette.

*Château
Sweet
Château*

To most, her life looked charming and grand,
but to Lucie it seemed that life was quite bland.

The Heiress from Paris had everything and more,
but thought that her life was a bit of a bore.

Upon awakening each day,
below *Eiffel* Tower,
Lucie played with Pompette
for nearly an hour.

In view of the city,
she exclaimed *"Bonjour Paris!"*
and then started the day with
her *Petite Chérie*.

Très Chic!

Always so chic, Lucie loved French fashion,
but she wished to discover her truest passion.

With a closetful of clothes and *Haute Couture* dresses,
she always wore black to avoid any guesses.

She adored makeup too and shiny lip gloss.
One swipe on her lips and a quick head toss!

Très Jolie!

Off to her salon,
new hairstyle, new day.
"*Mais Non!*" she exclaimed,
"The ponytail will stay!"

She was a girl of habit
but simply could not see,
that doing the same thing
put a bore in her *Belle Vie*.

Trop de parfums!

In the pink "fragrance room"
she chose her favorite scent.
A spritz of Lily *Rouge* for every event!

In the dining hall so grand
she had *Le Petit-Déjeuner*.
Two lavender *Macarons*
et une Café Au Lait.

Then off with Pompette through *Place de la Concorde*.
The same shopping each day left an heiress **BORED**.

Strolling through *Les Tuileries*,
Lucie wished for something that she could not see.

J'aime les fleurs!

The Heiress from Paris
had everything and more,
except for a life that she truly *J'adored.*

At *Place des Victoires* she met a painter,
who loved her style so much she asked to paint her.
Lucie looked at the portrait and said to her mate,
"I've always admired people who can create."

"I wish *I* could make something
to make people happy.
C'est la Vie Pompette,
Let's get a treat before you get yappy."

While pondering life
at *Le Petite Pâtisserie*,
Lucie said to Pompette, her dearest *amie*,

"I know what can bring a smile to my face,
La Maquillage boutique, my favorite place!"

J'adore macarons!

Lucie asked the clerk for her favorite lip gloss,
but the girl responded with a sad look of loss.

"They stopped making the gloss, so we cannot sell.
I'm sorry to say, my dear *Mademoiselle.*"

"*C'est TERRIBLE!*" Lucie cried
as she ran home feeling bad,
Sans favorite lip gloss, which made her quite sad.

The Heiress from Paris wished she had more,
and now she was ready for a comfy cozy snore.

That night in her bed
while turning and tossing,
Lucie dreamt when she made gloss
for her dolls of cake frosting.

She was creative, happy,
and had *Joi de Vivre.*
Making lip gloss for her dolls
gave her much glee.

Even though the heiress
was just a *Petite* girl of four,
life at the *Château* was never a bore.

The Heiress from Paris jumped out of the bed
    with a brilliant idea circling her head.
    "How could I forget my truest passion,
    and just live a life of following fashion?"

Magnifique!

"I've always loved playing makeup
    and making pastries, of course,
    I'll create a macaron lip gloss
    with my new secret sauce!"

Pompette looked around in a fit of wonder
as Lucie dashed to the kitchen as fast as thunder.

The heiress flung out every spoon, bowl and mixer.
Adding sugar and flour she stirred quicker and quicker!

After mixing for hours she applied the gloss to her lips,
as the liquid ran down the apron and onto her hips!

"*C'est Tout*, this macaron lip gloss is quite a mess!
It's *Horrible* in fact, I must confess."

"I give up!" the heiress said, and started to pout.
Pompette politely barked wanting to go out.

*Le Parc
s'il Vous Plait!*

Sucre

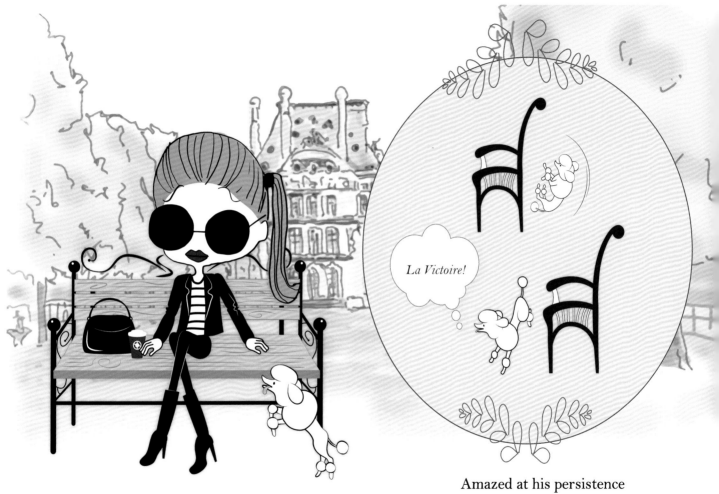

La Victoire!

Pompette started jumping over the bench but failed.
He tried again and again until he finally sailed.

Amazed at his persistence
and the lesson she was just taught,
Lucie rewarded Pompette at their favorite spot.

Lucie took a *Croissant* and gave him a bite,
"C'est Incroyable" she said, not believing the sight.

The crumbs on his whiskers were so plump and thick.
The butter from the pastry just made them stick!

"Butter!" yelled Lucie. "How could I forget?
This time, I will make it, even better yet!"

She mixed in the butter
and did not once stop,
until the batter looked rich
and creamy on top!

Lucie took the gloss and swiped it onto her lips,
and screamed with joy, "**NOT ONE DROP SLIPS**!"

Ooh la la

"Voilà!" Lucie screamed
as she danced in the air.
A new *Macaron* lip gloss
she would finally declare!

"I want to make people happy
and for them to feel pretty.
To keep the lip gloss for me
would just be a pity!"

Lucie hopped on her scooter
and gave the lip gloss away.
Sharing with others,
made life no longer *Blasé*.

The Heiress from Paris followed her dream,
even though it was not easy as it might've seemed.

In a Grand *Château* in the heart of Paris,
there lived a happy and creative heiress.
Her name was Lucie, and she found her passion,
instead of just shopping and following fashion.

La fin!

She created fabulous lipgloss, pastries, and more,
and never again thought her life was a bore...

Glossary

Château – home
Chic – stylish
Bonjour – hello
Petite Chérie – little sweetheart
Très Chic – very stylish
Haute Couture – high fashion
Très Jolie – very pretty
Mais Non – But No
Belle Vie – beautiful life
Lily Rouge – red lily
Trop de Parfum – too much perfume
Le Petit-Déjeuner – breakfast
Café au Lait – coffee with milk
J'adore les fleurs – I love the flowers
J'adored – loved
C'est La Vie – That's life

Le Petite Pâtisserie – small dessert
La Maquillage – makeup
J'adore macarons – I love macarons
Mademoiselle – young woman
Terrible – terrible, awful
Attendez Moi – wait for me
Joi de Vivre – joy of life
Magnifique – magnificent
C'est tout – That's all
Le Parc s'il vous plait – the park please
La Victoire – Victory
Croissant – French pastry
Incroyable – incredible
Voilà – here is
Blasé – unimpressed
La fin – the end

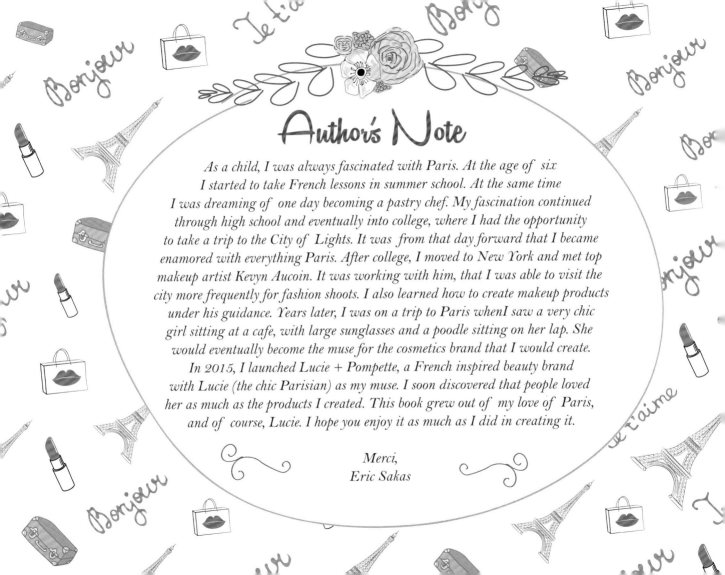

Author's Note

As a child, I was always fascinated with Paris. At the age of six
I started to take French lessons in summer school. At the same time
I was dreaming of one day becoming a pastry chef. My fascination continued
through high school and eventually into college, where I had the opportunity
to take a trip to the City of Lights. It was from that day forward that I became
enamored with everything Paris. After college, I moved to New York and met top
makeup artist Kevyn Aucoin. It was working with him, that I was able to visit the
city more frequently for fashion shoots. I also learned how to create makeup products
under his guidance. Years later, I was on a trip to Paris whenI saw a very chic
girl sitting at a cafe, with large sunglasses and a poodle sitting on her lap. She
would eventually become the muse for the cosmetics brand that I would create.
In 2015, I launched Lucie + Pompette, a French inspired beauty brand
with Lucie (the chic Parisian) as my muse. I soon discovered that people loved
her as much as the products I created. This book grew out of my love of Paris,
and of course, Lucie. I hope you enjoy it as much as I did in creating it.

Merci,
Eric Sakas